For Jill beside the sea – Mark Sperring
To our dear Aunty Janet – The Pope Twins

© 2006 The Chicken House

First published in the United Kingdom in 2006 by
The Chicken House, 2 Palmer Street, Frome, Somerset, BA11 1DS
www.doublecluck.com

Text © 2006 Mark Sperring
Illustrations © 2006 Liz and Kate Pope

Designed by Ian Butterworth
Printed and bound in China

British Library Cataloguing in Publication Data available
Library of Congress Cataloguing in Publication data available

HB ISBN: 1 904442 65 X
PB ISBN: 1 904442 98 6

Mermaid Dreams

Mark Sperring

Illustrated by

The Pope Twins

Chicken House

2 Palmer Street, Frome, Somerset BA11 1DS

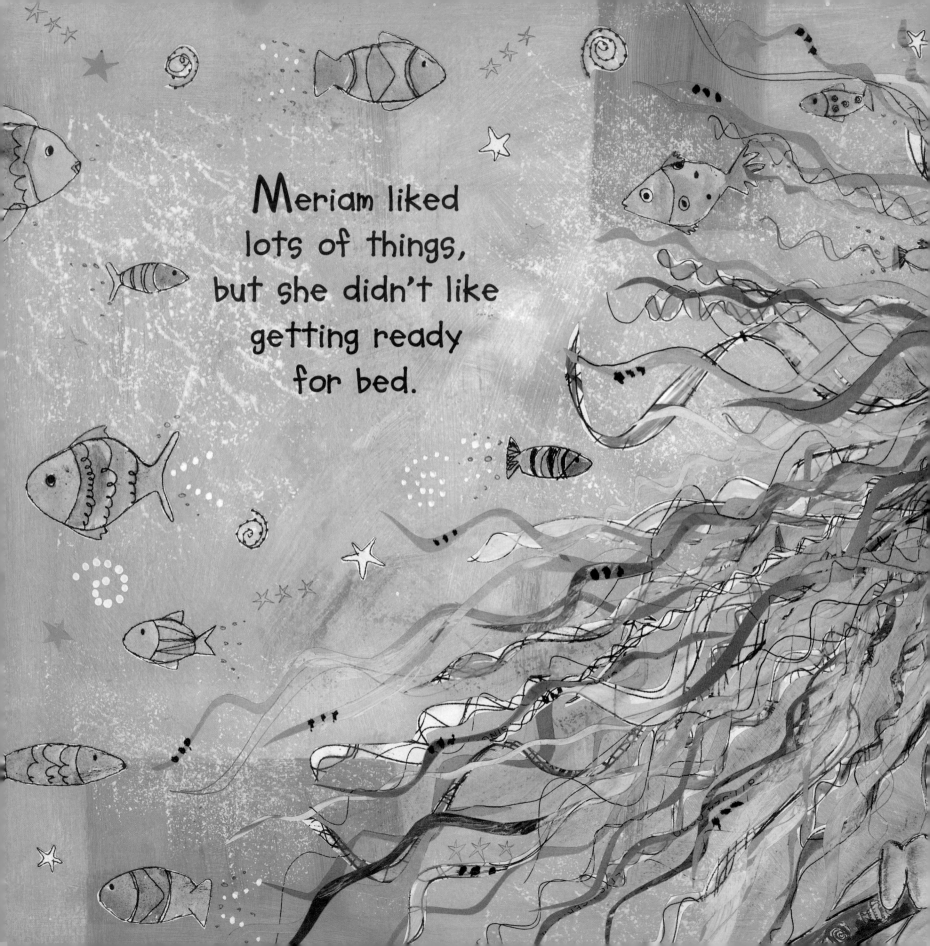

Meriam liked
lots of things,
but she didn't like
getting ready
for bed.

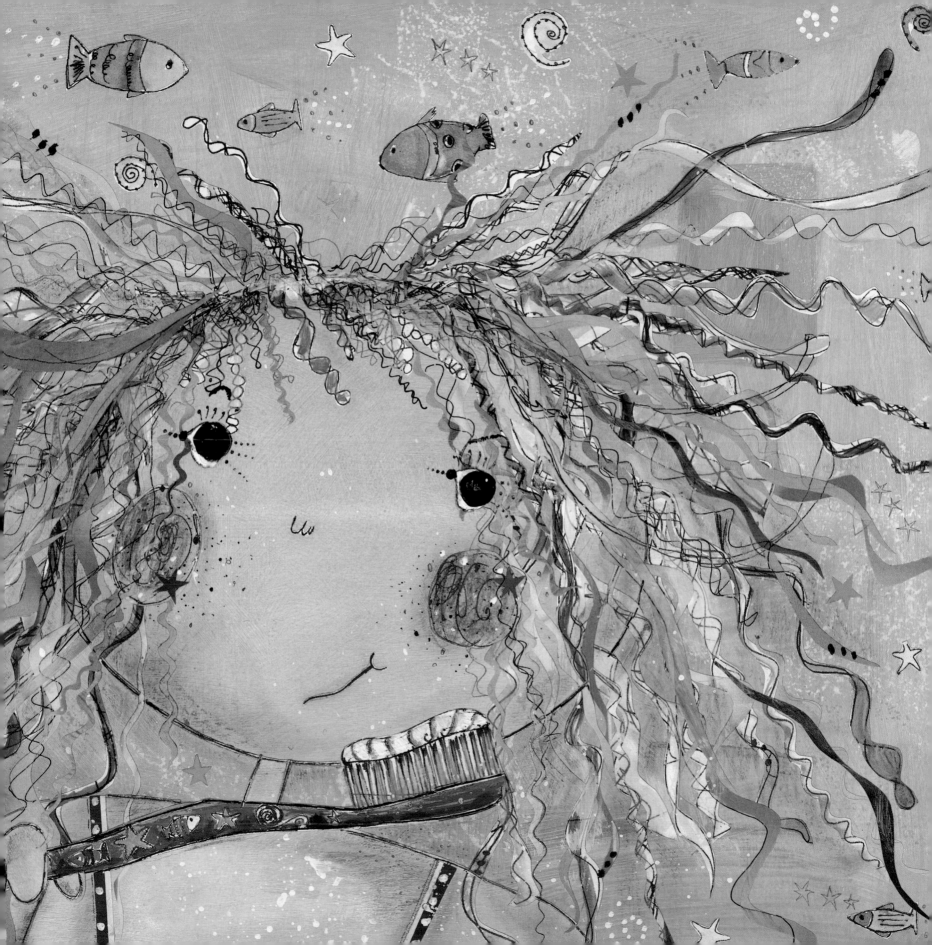

After she brushed her teeth, her mother always combed her tangled hair. One night as Meriam moaned and her mother combed, out fell a shell! 'Wherever did this come from?' asked Meriam's mother.

'I went to the beach today and lay in the sand,' said Meriam.

Her mother continued combing. 'Is your hair turning green?' she asked.

'It's a piece of seaweed,' said Meriam.

'I went in the ocean today
and dived beneath the waves.'

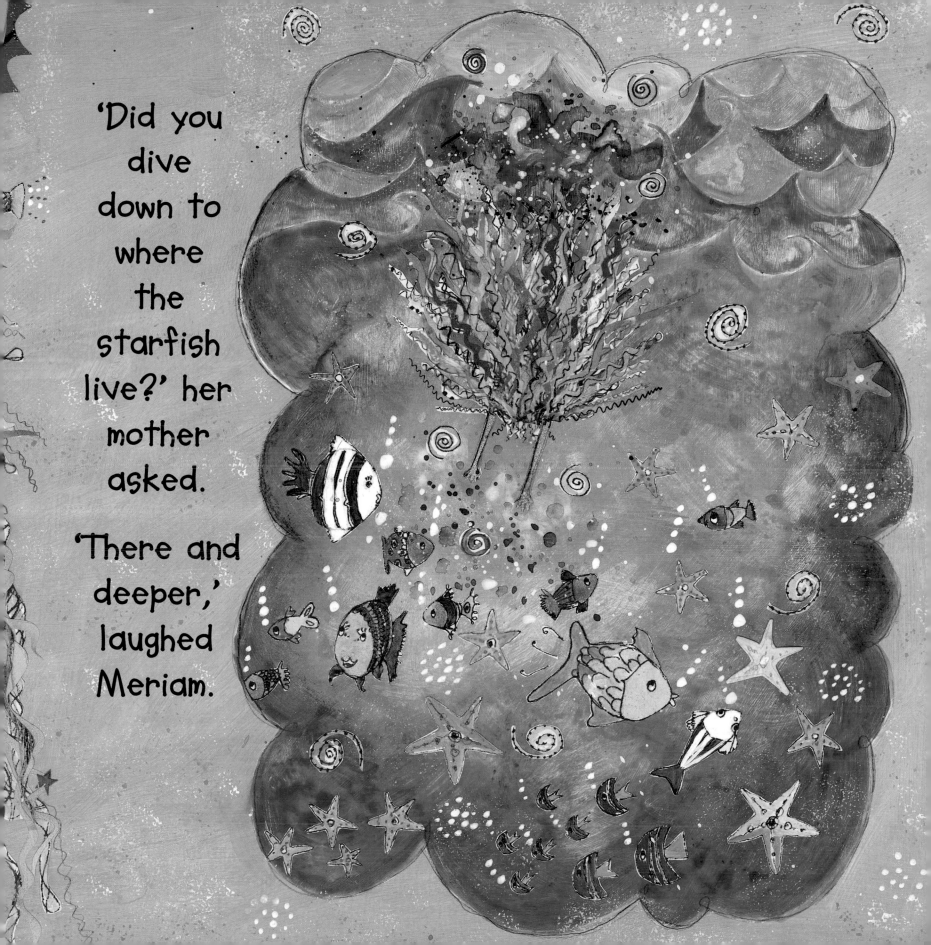

'Did you dive down to where the starfish live?' her mother asked.

'There and deeper,' laughed Meriam.

'Deeper than where the dolphins play. . .'

'Deeper than where the octopuses dance....'

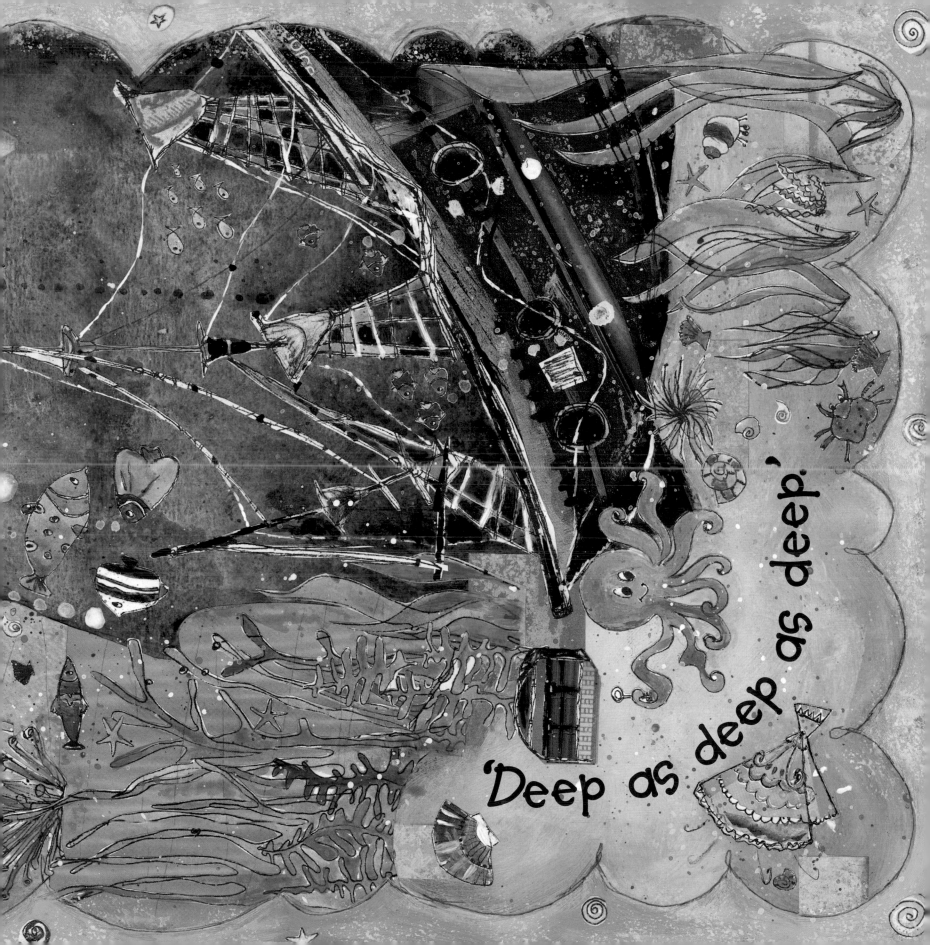

'Deep as deep as deep as deep.'

'To bring you the prettiest pearl!' Meriam smiled.

'Oh my,' gasped her mother.

'I was wondering,' asked Meriam, 'have I finished getting ready for bed?'

'No,' said her mother firmly.

Then Meriam's mother reminded her to 'clean out her ears' – and out jumped a little fish.

And to 'scrub behind her neck' —
and out scuttled a baby crab.
Finally, after all that getting ready...

Meriam was ready for bed.
'Sweet dreams,' her mother called.

At least she never had to clean between her toes!